The Biggest Surprise

Jadon And The Talking Trains

Author
Taneisha Pascoe-Matthews

Title book: The Biggest Surprise - Jadon and the Talking Trains
Author: Taneisha Pascoe-Matthews

© 2020, Taneisha Pascoe-Matthews
Self-Publishing
Onevoice.autism@gmail.com

Edited by Janice Thomas

Designed by Taneisha Pascoe-Matthews

Additional script supporters: Sherika Boothe-Clarke,
Dean Brown-Richmond and Fran Nantongwe

Illustrated by Sameer Kassar

Dear Reader,
You are amazing.
You are kind.
You are smart.
You are unique.
You are a friend.

This book belongs to _____

Written in dedication to Jadon and Ethan.

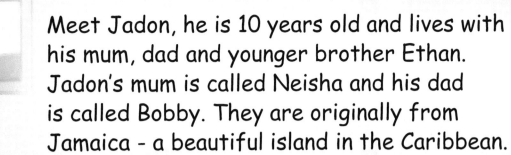

Meet Jadon, he is 10 years old and lives with his mum, dad and younger brother Ethan. Jadon's mum is called Neisha and his dad is called Bobby. They are originally from Jamaica - a beautiful island in the Caribbean.

Jadon is autistic, but he is so much more. He is handsome, smart, caring, friendly, energetic and is fun to be around. He likes baking chocolate cake with his mum as well as watching and memorizing YuVube videos.

Jadon likes many things, but he really loves trains. He has a large collection with different colours, sizes and shapes. He sometimes shares with his younger brother Ethan, but often they get into sibling fights, as Jadon is protective of his trains.

Jadon was born in the lovely city of Norwich, on a beautiful Summer's day. Jadon lived in Norwich for three years before the family moved to London. It was while living in Norwich that his parents discovered he was autistic, just before turning 3 years old.

One day, Jadon and his family were relaxing in the living room. It was the calm period between the family dinnertime and bedtime. Ethan was colouring and his mum and dad were watching TV.

Suddenly, you could see a broad smile on Jadon's face. He was watching video clips of trains, when a train popped up that he did not know. He continued watching and the smile got wider and wider.

Jadon was not yet talking but he had many ways of communicating. He had spent the last five years getting support from a speech therapist, his teachers, teaching assistants, his parents and his friends.

Jadon was now three months from his 8th birthday, but over the years he found other ways to make his needs known. He would sometimes take his mother and father by their hands, hand them a picture card to make a request, type a message on his iPad or sign using Makaton.

You could tell he was ready to let his parents know about the trains! Jadon's fingers were moving quickly, and it helped that he was good at spelling. He was now standing in front of his mum and dad with a message that read "I have found some new trains, can I have them please?"

Neisha looked at Bobby with the "We are not buying another train glare". Bobby said, "Jadon, you don't need more trains, you have more than enough."

Jadon typed another message. This time it read, "Please, these are new, I have never seen these before." Jadon was now switching his attention from the iPad to his parents like a flashing light on a Christmas tree. Neisha and Bobby had a quick little whisper to themselves.

Neisha turned to Jadon and said, "We can get the new trains, but you must promise to share with your little brother Ethan." Jadon was not always happy to share his trains with Ethan, especially his favourite Kingston blue train. This time Jadon used the Makaton sign for 'yes' and he signed it five times.

Jadon's dad said, "Ok, on Saturday when we are in town, we will visit your favourite toy store." Jadon could not stop smiling that evening.

Bright and early on Saturday, Jadon was the first one up. After having breakfast and completing the morning chores, they all got ready and headed to the mall.

Jadon was extremely excited; he was finally going to get the new trains he wanted. He had been watching all their videos since they popped up on his iPad earlier that week.

As the car drove into the shopping mall car park, you could see the toy store; it was next to a cafe on the ground floor. Jadon knew the store very well; he had visited the shop many times before. This was not your usual toy store.

With the car parked, Jadon waited with excitement for the door to be opened.

Growing up, Jadon was not always aware of his surroundings and would open doors without looking and bumped into people while being out.

The family got to the toy store early to avoid the busy period. It is usually buzzing with families in the afternoons. Jadon is sometimes affected by loud noises, even though his mum and dad would always joke that he seemed to be ok in noisy toy shops.

As they entered the store, Bobby turned to Jadon and said, "Remember you always need to be close to us." Jadon signed, 'yes dad', as he walked by a big green dinosaur. Jadon was focused on getting to the train aisle. Nothing was going to distract him at this point.

They started checking the train aisle for the new trains. They looked for almost ten minutes, but Jadon's special trains were nowhere to be found.

Jadon's mum had an idea. "Let's ask one of the workers," she said. Jadon handed his iPad with pictures of the new trains to the attendant. He took a quick look and started to shake his head. It was not looking positive.

The attendant turned to Jadon and said, "I am sorry young man but those are no longer made for sale." Jadon sighed disappointingly followed by a loud exhale.

It was not what Jadon was hoping for and was clearly looking sad. His mum gave him a hug followed by his dad. They thanked the shop attendant for his help and left the store to continue the other activities planned for the day in town.

Later that evening when Jadon and Ethan were asleep, his dad had an idea. "Let's try one of those online stores, maybe there is someone selling old toys," he said. They were searching for almost thirty minutes, when suddenly they saw the trains Jadon wanted on the popular website AMIZON.

They quickly made the purchase and asked for the trains to be delivered the following day. They decided they were not going to let Jadon know before the arrival of the trains. They wanted it to be a big surprise!

The next morning Jadon was up a little later than normal. Even so, he went to check that all his trains were in the exact location he left them before going to bed the previous night. This was part of Jadon's routine and he was able to tell if they had been moved.

The doorbell started ringing. "It must be the delivery," said his mum. It was the package they were awaiting, but they were not ready to show Jadon. They wanted to add the new batteries they had bought first.

Jadon was in the living room, so his dad went to the kitchen and quickly added the batteries. They now needed the perfect moment to surprise Jadon with the trains.

The door pushed open, and Jadon walked in. His dad tried to hide them, but his hand touched a button and the long green train started talking. "My name is Mark," said the train, "I am ready to go." Astonished, Jadon looked at his dad and mum with the biggest smile on his face. James the blue train said, "Let's go Mark".

"Wow, this is amazing!", said Jadon's mother. "These are some awesome trains." They all walked to the living room to add them to Jadon's train mat.

Jadon and his dad placed all the trains on the mat, and they all sat to watch Jadon getting to know his new trains. What happened next was the biggest surprise of the day.

Luke the blue train said, "Who will join me with this load". "I C-A-N!", said Jadon. His mum and dad looked at each other with their mouths wide open. "Did you hear that?", asked his mum in disbelief.
Well let's go, we have to be quick", said Luke. "I A-M R-EA-DY", said Jadon.

His parents froze; they wanted to say something, but they did not want to interrupt. They continued listening to Jadon and The Talking Trains.

Neisha and Bobby were so happy to hear Jadon's sweet voice. They all hugged, cried, laughed and rejoiced. They were aware that while most autistic people speak very well, some don't speak, and many start talking later. It was a moment they had hoped for.

That was the day Jadon started talking and now he just does not stop. Jadon even kept his promise of sharing the trains with Ethan, well mostly.

Printed in Great Britain
by Amazon